# RED BIKE

By

Caridad Svich

*Santa Catalina Editions edition*
*An imprint of NoPassport Press*

*RED BIKE* copyright 2017, 2018, 2019 by Caridad Svich

All rights reserved. Except for brief passages quoted in newspaper, magazine, radio, or television reviews, no part of this book may be reproduced in any form or by any means, electronic or mechanical, without permission in writing from the author. Professionals and amateurs are hereby warned that this material, being fully protected under the Copyright Laws of the United States of America and of all the other countries of the Berne and Universal Copyright Conventions, is subject to royalty. All rights including, but not limited to professional, amateur, recording, motion picture, recitation, lecturing, public reading, radio and television broadcasting, and the rights of translation into foreign languages are expressly reserved. Emphasis is placed on the question of readings and all uses of this play by educational institutions, permission for which must be secured from the author and her representatives.

New Dramatists Alumni, 424 West 44th Street, NY, NY 10036 USA,

e-mail: newdramatists@newdramatists.org, and e-mail: csvich21@caridadsvich.com

Santa Catalina Editions/NoPassport imprint; www.nopassport.org

**ISBN: 978-0-359-65874-9**

# RED BIKE

A play

By Caridad Svich

RED BIKE is a 2018 through 2019 National New Play Network (NNPN) rolling world premiere with theatres PYGmalion Productions (Salt Lake City, Utah), Simpatico Theatre (Philadelphia, PA), Know Theatre (Cincinnati, Ohio), and The Wilbury Group (Providence, Rhode Island).

The play was developed at the Lark and New Dramatists in New York City and with Chaskis Theatre in London, England (UK).

Along its development, it was also read at Smith College, Flint Youth Theatre in Michigan, Unicorn Theatre in Kansas City, Jackalope Theatre in Chicago, and the 2017 NNPN National Showcase of New Plays at Orlando Shakespeare Festival, and presented at Jedlicka Performing Arts Center at Morton College in Illinois.

RED BIKE is the first in a seven-play cycle of plays, which includes *FUEL, Hurt Song,* and *Holler River.*

## RED BIKE
## Production Credits- PYGmalion Theatre

RED BIKE premiered with PYGmalion Theatre Company (Fran Pruyn, Artistic Director) in Salt Lake City, Utah at the Rose Wagner Center on April 20, 2018.

The cast was as follows:

Sydney Shoell

Jesse Nepivoda

Andrea Peterson


Director: Fran Pruyn
Assistant Director: Madeleine Rex
Stage Manager: Jennie Pett
Costume Designer: Teresa Sanderson
Sound Designer: Troy Klee
Lighting Designer: Molly Tiede
Scenic Designer: Thomas George

## RED BIKE- Production Credits- Simpatico Theatre

RED BIKE premiered with Simpatico Theatre (Allison Heishman, Artistic Director) in Philadelphia, PA at the Caplan Studio Theatre on June 6, 2018.

### The cast was as follows:

Torez Mosley

Wilfredo Amill

Emily R. Johnson

Directed by Sam Tower
Asst. Director Nia Benjamin
Communiturg Zandra King
Stage Manager Melody Wong
Asst. Stage Manager Franny Mestrich

Music Composed and Performed by
Jordan Micah Merrill McCree and Andrew Nittoli

Sound Design and Engineered by Damien Figueras

Scenic Design Petra Floyd
Lighting Design Angela Myers
Costume Design Tara Webb
Technical and Production: Lauren Tracy, Joe Daniels and Andrew J. Cowles
Production Photography: Daniel Kontz.

RED BIKE- Production Credits- Know Theatre

RED BIKE premiered with Know Theatre (Andrew Hungeford, Artistic Director) in Cincinnati, OH on February 12, 2019.

The cast was as follows:

Montez O. Jenkins-Copeland

Maliyah Gramata-Jones

Directed by Holly Derr

RED BIKE- Production Credits- Wilbury Group

RED BIKE premiered with Wilbury Group (Josh Short, Artistic Director) in Providence, RI on February 21, 2019

The cast was as follows:

Sarah Leach
Marcel Mascaro
Allison Lewis-Towbes
Phoenyx Williams
Jason Quinn

Directed by Kate Bergstrom

## RED BIKE

So, it's like this: you're eleven years old, you live in a small town and the times are dark, as they say. But you have a bike, a bike you love, a bike that makes you dream about a world bigger than the one you live in. One day you take a ride through the outer edges of your town and something goes awry. Let's call it an accident. Let's say it causes you to see the world anew. Or maybe it just causes you to see the world for what it truly is.

## RED BIKE Cast and text breakdown:

A play for one or more performers.

The performer(s) may be any gender and age (from late teens and above). Casting, however, must be inclusive and reflective of the world.

If the play is cast with three-four performers, then they may alternate stanzas, and speak at times in unison. An intergenerational cast is preferred. But actors need not be all the same gender, ethnic, orientation or racial identity.

The speaker in the text is a child of eleven years of age and their adult self, reflecting back on themselves as a child. No attempt should be made to make the performer "appear" to be a child in affect or clothing. We know how to play pretend. Get on with it.

All the text in the play is spoken, except for stage directions in parentheses.

This play is divided into 50 discrete frames or chapters, each of which could be seen as a micro shift in the play's universe.

In other words, it is possible that after each chapter, there is an extended breath, a suspension, or a silence.

Or perhaps

A movement sequence

Or a dance break

Or just being with the audience in light

Sharing the space for a moment,

Before the next section begins.

# 1

You want it. You dreamt about it. You have it.

The red bike

You saw it in the window

It smiled at you

You knew it

You two were meant to be

'Cause this is not just any bike

This is the RED BIKE

The one that when you go down the street, everyone will see you

Everyone will stop, and say, heeeey, red bike

Envy

That's right

You will inspire envy

You know about this

Because you've been learning about envy for a long time

Even though you're only eleven

Envy is in your bones

It's the cool sneaks and the amazing car and the kick-ass tech device


Your parents talk about things like this

Only they use different words


Your parents talk about the things they want

The things they're told they must want to be good citizens, to be good people

Your parents work hard

They have ten jobs but they say they have two

They pretend they're happy

But they're anxious

You see them


They rub their temples

They hide their smiles

They put the bread away in the bread basket

And 'Don't dunk it in the eggs'

Even though they want to

Even though it's yummy to eat eggs sunny side up

      Or over easy, as my dad says

And dunk, dunk, dunk the bread

And slop up the gooey yellow mess

They know better

They watch their cholesterol

They watch their clocks

They watch the news

And get red in the face

And let their anger go to their shoes

To their stomach

To their knees

Shoulders

Neck

They say 'we're fine'

They say

Go on now

Go for a ride

See ya later

Make sure you lock up the bike if you stop somewhere


They say these things

Because they know what these things mean


They say these things

Because the news is bad

And chaotic and depressing and confusing

And makes them feel like they don't know anything

About how the world works

And how they're going to pay their bills next month


My parents wish they didn't have bills

They wished they owned things

Real things

That last

**2**

    Like that Guy in the center of town

That owns all those buildings and the airport and the park

And the water supply

And other things too

Invisible things

Like stocks and derivatives and securities


I heard him once

He was talking on the phone

Really loud

Near the luxury condo he built


The luxury condo with the FOR LEASE sign

The luxury condo that's been empty for months

But people say is all bought up

All bought up by other people in other countries in other cities

Who are these people?

Will we ever get to meet them?


3


      I don't know half of our neighbors

This town is moving so fast

It's like lightning

That's what my dad says


I wish I knew what he meant

Like, how can earth and rock and concrete and brick and steel and glass

Move

Like

Lightning?


But I believe him

'cause he knows things

He has five jobs when he says he has two

And he's been working his whole life

Gets up at 5 AM

Goes to the warehouse

You know it

You've seen it

It's just up the road

It's HUGE

It's the WAAAAAREHOUSE

It's where the ol' corn field used to be

Or maybe it was wheat?

4

      Back in the day, the Ol' Guy says

      When we're on the bus

Back in the day this all here was growing

I'm, like, okay

Back in the day, we made things, the ol' guy says

And he gets a catch in his throat

And I think he's gonna cry

And get all meepy

Like in one of those stupid movies or something

But he doesn't

He just says, 'way of things

Just the way things are now

5

   My dad's been working in that warehouse

Ever since I can remember

He moves boxes around

Orders that come in

Stuff that gets shipped out

He says the warehouse is full of stuff from floor to ceiling

Piles of stuff that all sorts of people want

And need to get NOW

All that stuff?

    He says, yeah

That's a hella lotta stuff

    He says, yeah

    And they're building another warehouse a couple miles down

Filled with more stuff to ship out?

    He says, yeah

I'm, like, hell
What we gonna do with all that stuff?

    Make people happy

## 6

    When people ask me what my dad does
And what my mom does

I say, they make people happy

I figure it's as good an answer as any

People don't really want to know about some warehouse

Or some store or some clinic or some school

Where people do basic things

Everyday impossible things

Cuz it just makes them think about stuff

Like, how they're gonna pay their bills

And how the insurance keeps going up

And how everyone says everything is fine

But they can't get their breakfast sandwich

At that place anymore, cuz it got shut down

And when the hell is something else gonna open up there?

Man, that place has been empty for, like, ever

I hear them

I know

Like, when I'm on my bike

I'm, like, a radar

Or a drone or something

7

       I see them sometimes

The drones

Dude says they're planes

But I'm, like, no way, man, they're drones

Can't you tell?

What movies you been watching?

Drones everywhere, man

Watching us

Keeping our secrets

Making a mess of everything over there

Seen the news?

        No. I don't watch the news. Nothing to do with me

You jokin', right, Dude?

        Listen, I don't got time for this

And we stop watching the sky

And I get back on my bike

And dude heads down the road

To the ol' dollar store that's a two-dollar store now

I think dude's messed up

The news got something to do with something

'cause why else would it make everyone like a fuse?

8

        The FOR LEASE sign

Is gleaming

The guy's wearing a suit


It was hot

Not like today

But still hot

And I thought he must be sweating like a pig in that suit


Like that cartoon on Saturday morning

The one with the guy with the gun

And the stupid animals running around looking for food


*Stocks and derivatives and securities*


It's like he was chanting

Like he was praying to some god

'cause he kept looking up at the sky


I thought that's the guy

That's the guy that owns half of this town

That's the guy that cut down all of the trees

He looked at me

Red bike

I could see it on his face

He wanted it too

*Red bike, red bike, red-*

I turned the corner

He went back to looking at the sky

*Stocks and derivatives and securities*

That guy is smart

He has a vision

Everyone says so

A vision of the world

9

I have visions too

But I don't tell anybody

'cause people don't wanna hear from some kid

They're, like, go on now

Go for a ride

See ya later

I wish I could tell them

I wish I could tell them what I see

But it's hot

And I'm sweaty

And the air is murder

And I'm thinking that if I don't get to that hill over there I'm meat

'cause the hill is where you get the best ride

The hill is where you see the whole city

10

> I am so sweaty

I shouldn't have worn these clothes

I'm so stupid sometimes

My legs are giving out, too

I am so not cut out for a marathon

I dream about it sometimes

Like, if I were on the tour de France n shit

I know you need a whole lotta money n sponsorship n stuff

And, like, they're all on dope

But still…

Riding through those hills

Up those curves

Winding up and down those roads

In the rain

In the sun

Past the trees and the dog shit

Man oh man, wouldn't it just be…

**11**

Dreams and visions are two different things

I know

The ol' guy on the bus told me

He said his great-great-something or other

Went on this vision quest

Totally for real

Went out to where that abandoned silo is now

Way, way out, out past the warehouse and the Waffle Stop

Went out there with no food, no nothing

Freaky-ass cold at night

And prayed

For his family and his friends and who knows what else

Cried like a baby just born

Eyes like rain

For days and days

And nights and more days

Got sick, too

Got all kinds of everything

Bugs biting

Earth creaking

Waffle Stop sign blinking through the core of night

Thought: this is death

This is where I meet you, my friend

And then outta nowhere

Some kind of animal

Come outta shadow and light

Looking like it'd seen better days

Like it had lived the past of another animal

And had come back in a new shape

Stood near the silo

Eyes like fire

Song in its throat

Something about smallness and rage n chaos in the belly

Animal stared

Night fell like seven moons

Freaky as hell

But the ol' guy's great-great something or other

Stayed

With the animal

Through the night

And another day

Until there was no sound

Just light

And an amazing kinda wonder

Like the weight of the world

Was dancing with them

Like in some disco or something

Thump, thump, thump

Dancing its heaviness through the body

Animal beams


Great-great something or other laughs

Rain down both their faces

They can't  stop  dancing

Can't  stop  moving

Voice calls out from somewhere, hey, you, where'd you get that joy?


And then nothing

Like the silo is just the silo


And the Waffle Stop sign is making that kinda buzzy sound

That neon sometimes makes


And it's just cold

And here

**12**

      The hill's not that far

I can see it now

My legs are starting to find themselves again

Still hot, though

Why is it so hot this time of year?

Shouldn't be this way

Dad says it was never like this when he was a kid

Mom says she don't remember

Everybody's screwed up about the weather these days

Even dude says spring is gone


The news is killing us, someone says

Drone flies past


I just want to be a good person

Hell, I got a red bike

The same red bike I stared at through the window

Same red bike my parents said I had to wait for

'Til that check come in

And that other check come in

And that lottery ticket give us five dollars extra


And I know, I know it's made in some other country far away

But what the hell am I supposed to do?

Like, they don't make it here anymore

That company shut down years ago

Somebody gotta make red bikes somewhere

So kids like me can dream


**13**

      On the hill now

Man, it is something, right?

The whole town is looking at me

Hey all. Look here. See.

Envy

Sometimes it feels good

Sometimes you wanna revel in it

Look at me

Look at me

Look. At. Me.

> *(And maybe something physically astonishing occurs. An act of daring and ecstatic joy.)*

**14**

Something sticks

On the ground

Greasy

I am moving

Fast

Hella fast

Down this hill

Brake. Come on. Brake.

I've been down this hill a million times.

What the hell is going on?

Brake. Come on. Brake.

The hill is taking me

This is wrong

This is doom

I'll never make the tour de France now

I'll be like that biker in the Olympics

The one who went careening off the road

Crash splat

And lay there crying like a pup

Knees and legs and arms smashed to shit

Pity

I will inspire pity

Not envy

What is the world coming to?

Brake. Come on. Brake.

It's gonna be all pain now

Get ready for the inevitable, friend

It's just you and the hill and the red bike

Going

Hell

Knows

Where

**15**

    What's that?

Bird? Squirrel? Rabbit?

Am I gonna be a murderer now?

Move outta the way of the way, animal

    I'm holding onto the handlebars as if life

MOVE OUT

Mirage

Am seeing things now

Breath races

Heart pumps

Three hundred billion seconds per minute

Thump thump thump

Like at a bad disco or something

I'm thinking about my math homework

I'm thinking about Dude

And how I promised I'd help out with their band

I'm thinking 'bout the grass that needs mowin'

And the dirty laundry I stuffed in the back of the closet

And how I told mom and dad I'd be home before dark

The world is gonna eat me aliiiiive

**16**

      Panic

Panic is the worst

Panic is not a superhero move

And we're superheroes, right?

What'd Dude and I swear to each other back in school?

We are superheroes

Just stay calm

Focused

Alert

In the zone

Be in the zone

Zen

What's Zen?

How do I get Zen?

Heart pumps like a mad fist

Beads of sweat on my forehead nose lips

This is not looking good

I'm gonna die

I'm gonna die on this stupid hill


**17**

      Wait

This can't be the end

I just started

I'm just a kid

I got my whole life

I've been through plenty of shit before

I've been through hella stuff

Like, when I fell in the backyard

On that steel thing

And got all those stitches

That took weeks of healing

And it was nice, right?

It was ice cream and staying in bed

And being sick from school

And people visiting and calling

And asking about me all the time

I was a star

I was a superstar

It was great

I am a superstar

What the hell am I worried about?

This is just a road

This is just a bike moving way too fast

So what? I can handle it

I can handle anything

## 18

      My mom handles six jobs even though she says she has two

And she still has time to be a mom

And do things

And ask me how I'm doing

Sometimes she even gives me a kiss on the forehead

And just looks at me

Like I'm the most special person in the whole world

She does all that

When I know she cries sometimes

I've seen her

That time in the dollar store

She was crying in aisle nine

Next to the laundry detergent and the toilet cleaner

She didn't see me

I had a bag of skittles in my hand

Wanted to ask her if we could…

But when I saw her

I just

Shoved the skittles back onto the shelf in aisle five

Later, in the car, on the way home

I touched the back of her neck

Like, it's okay, mom

Whatever it is, it'll be okay

She didn't say nothing

But she smiled

And put music on


Something really stupid on the radio

All those heartbreak songs

Mom loves them

She started singing at the top of her lungs

Roll the window down

Make some NOIIIIIISE


*(And the kid sings about the last chorus and 15-30 seconds of the "say that you'll love me" section of the pop song "Unbreak my Heart" by Toni Braxton, full out, as if singing along to the radio until they are interrupted by a rush of)*

## 19

Air's like a tunnel

Like it don't even exist now

I'm just flesh and wheels


Even the road's gone

Must be someone laughing somewhere

Isn't that what Dude says their people say?

When shit goes down, someone must be laughing somewhere

I'm like a cartoon

The one where the animal is on the scooter

Hits a rock in the road

And flips up into the air

A gazillion times

Head wobbling

Teeth chattering

Body parts moving every which way

Boing boing boing

Look at that thing go

Animal starts dreaming of the ol' days

Back when life was easy as pie

Sit in a hammock

Rock to some sweet music

Kick up your feet

And think of the future

**20**

When I was five I made a list

Of everything I wanted to be

Superstar pirate astronaut helicopter ice cream maker diver climber builder ninja warrior movie-maker Oscar winner Nobel winner Olympics winner scientist athlete inventor history teacher philosopher poet shaman singer leader fire-breather lion beast unicorn[1]

My parents said lists make us wish for the impossible

They're unrealistic

STOP MAKING LISTS

---

[1] This list could be longer. It is encouraged in rehearsal to ask the performers and members of creative team to add to this list from their own childhood perspectives. It is also possible to ask the audience to contribute to the list, if the staging allows for organic interaction.

But I didn't listen


Superstar pirate astronaut helicopter ice cream maker diver climber builder ninja warrior movie-maker Oscar winner Nobel winner Olympics winner scientist athlete inventor history teacher philosopher poet shaman singer leader fire-breather lion beast unicorn


I'd seen mom and dad make lists

And not just for groceries n shit

But for next year and the year after that


All kinds of dreaming


'Bout taking trips

And buying a house

And owning things


One list was just appliances

Another list was cities

Are we moving? I ask

They don't say

But I can see them thinking

    Whole lotta towns we could be in

I make a face

    Don't look at us like that, kid

    We know some things 'bout things

I say, yeah

But in my heart I know better

**21**

    I've seen them come back from all those wars

And they sure looked like they needed a big-time list

A new list to start their lives

Or make them up again

And I thought if I ever gotta go to some war

Fight for hell knows what

*Stocks and derivatives and securities*

I'd sure as hell make me a list

'cause even if there's no future

Even if they're just five people left in your town

'You gotta make things mean something

Hell yeah'

**22**

      Ol'' guy says people back in his town

Back in the middle of the middle of the country

They're all old

Like, real old

And they're all men, too

Old, old guys sitting in some town

Watching it die

I ask ol' guy on the bus, what do they do?

He says they talk about the old days

Talk about how they didn't do nothing for their town

But let everybody go

All the young ones couldn't wait to leave

So, they said

Go on now

Go for a ride

See ya later

Except they didn't come back

'cause there was nothing to come back to

And pretty soon it was just them

Buy the bread and milk at the lil' store

Eat pizza at the diner on Saturdays

Drink at the bar for hours and a day

Watch their loved ones die

Bury them in the lil cemetery

And wait

Wait

Until they're gone

And the whole town

Vanishes

Right along with them


What was the name of that town?


    Hamburger.


I say to ol' guy, are you shitting me?

That town's called Hamburger?


    Ol' guy says watch your language

    How old are you anyway, kid?


Eleven

Eleven's too young for curse words

Who made them rules?

People

What people gotta do with words? Aren't words just words?

Ol' guy says his ol' town is dead and he don't wanna talk about it no more

Hamburger

I got a mind to look up that town and call his bluff

But I can see ol' guy thinking

His brow creases

Gets a far-away look in his eyes

He left his town, too, you see

He was one of the young ones

And now he's old

And he's here

And I bet he's thinking one day

One day this town is gonna die

And is he gonna watch it happen?

Gets all angry for a second

And says

> That guy, that guy who's bought half this town
>
> He's gonna ruin it for all of us
>
> No trees anymore
>
> Just condos
>
> Steel and glass
>
> Where are we gonna live?
>
> Where are we gonna go?

Hamburger.

> He makes a face

23

But then

We start laughing

Both of us

Silly kid laughing

Baby laughing

Giggling hiccupping roaring

Like we both ate the best hamburger in our lives

All juicy and melt-y and smelling like fire n onions n hickory smoke

And we're tellin' the whole world about it on some commercial somewhere

I LOVE THIS PLACE

I LOVE WHERE I AM

I'M GONNA SAVE THIS TOWN

FROM ALL OF THE STEEL AND GLASS AND BULL-SHIT

BRING BACK THE TREES

PLANT SOME SEEDS

KEEP YOUR FAITH IN THIS TOWN

I'm thinking with talk like this

Man oh man, we could run for some office somewhere

We could be SUPERSTARS

**24**

      So, I've basically stopped looking at the road

I'm letting the bike do what it does

If my superhero powers don't kick in

Then I'm facing the biggest most spectacular crash

In this town's history

Make the evening news

Make the headlines

Go viral

Maybe I'll get a book made out of my life

Or a movie

Or a series

Or a video

Or a song

Three minutes of a song can change a person's life

Isn't that what they say?

I'll be that person

The one in the song

THE KID WITH THE RED BIKE

People will pray to me

Send flowers to me

Light candles in my name

Forever young

25

      Man, this shit is messed up

Like, we all wanna be famous

But not like that

Not for some accident

Hell, they'll just say I was stupid for even going down this hill

And forget all about me

I'll be like that curse in that story

Don't mention the kid with the red bike

They're bad news

Bad juju

## 26

      Breeze

Faint as anything

But it feels good

Like hope

**27**

      I wanna call somebody

But I got nothing on me

It's just me and the bike


How I'm still on this thing

Is like a miracle


Should've crashed by now

Should be on the road pavement grass

Splitting my nose lips knees


If I were the ol' guy

I'd say this got something to do with the gods


If I were Dude

I'd say this got something to do with my natural superhero moves

If I were my mom and dad

I'd say I am

GROUNDED

For weeks

Not that my mom and dad don't believe in miracles

But they're more practical than that

Like, they go to church and talk to people

And make nice on Sundays

But they've seen too much of the world

To believe in grace

I mean, you can ask 'em

But I'd bet you anything they'd say no

Before they'd give you the party line

They're honest like that

28

        Sometimes

Sometimes

I think about the gods

Way up there

And the ones down below too


And all of the mess they get themselves in

Like, way bigger messes than us


And it's like, envy, you know

Monster envy

Like, deep


cuz I'd like to hang out with them

And stir things up


Just to see if I could

Just to see if I'd last


**29**

    Some gods die slow deaths

Before they become super gods

Like that guy who got chained to a rock

He was a god, right?

And he totally got the shit kicked out of him

If it wasn't for that kid that got sent to that island

To ask him all of those questions bout fire n stuff

He woulda never made it to super god

I mean, I don't think I'm a super god

But it'd be fun, right?

To walk round all proud

Thinking I got some connection to things

Thinking I got some lineage

30

      Ol' guy used that word once: lineage

It made me smile

'cause I could see how it made him look up and out

I said, man, that's a big ass word

      He looks at me, you cursin' again?

I was, like, just words

      What have your people been teaching you?

Stuff

      What kinda stuff?

Stuff bout stuff

Ol' guy got all serious

And said lineage was not something to make a mockery of

'cause it's our bloodlines and the songs we got inside

And the fires too

And the little aches we pretend not to notice

Except when we feel them late at night

And our chest is just about bustin' outta itself


He said lineage tells us who we are

N who we could be too


cuz maybe somewhere in our line

There was someone that never did what they set out to do

But they dreamt about it

And their dreaming got inside you when you were born


So that when you're on the road

Clinging to the handlebars like life

You think the tour de France IS possible

IS something you were made for

**31**

    So are the dreams you got

'Bout someday owning a house

Not a big house

Just enough to not have to worry 'bout rent all the time

And payin' everybody everything every month

And seein' how you're gonna stretch things til Tuesday, like my dad says

You could even maybe get a nice outfit

Just to walk round and feel good 'bout things

And maybe get that little elephant mom likes so much

From that antique store down in that village we went to once

And eat ice cream made with jasmine and roses

And feel all peaceful

Like the world's a good place

N you're doing good by it

And maybe sing a little song too

'cause it's nice to sing sometimes

*(sung, very simply, almost to self)*

I am here

I am here

Look out, world. I am here

*(Back to…)*

Breeze comes at you

As you speed down the hill

Happy

Like, for real, happy

32

You remember that time you went to that famous theme park

That everyone swore was the happiest place ever

It made you anxious

And it made your mom and dad n everyone else crazy anxious

You felt so empty when you walked outta there

Like someone had dug a hole in your heart

And all this misery was just oozing outta you

And you wanted to shout

All of your sadness

Into the sky

And you thought I HATE THIS PLACE

I hate someone tellin me I gotta be happy all the time

I hate feelin like I can't buy all the stuff I want

While that stupid lady with the white hair and the killer boots

Spent five hundred dollars on that ONE THING

'cause she could

'cause it made her feel more important than everyone else

In the whole entire store

And how you want to shout at her

CALL HER OUT

And tell her she was the stupidest person in the world

'cause her stuck-up-ness was just shit

And it was so gonna catch up with her someday

When she was lookin outta her luxury condo

At the plaza with no trees

Feeling all alone

'cause that ONE THING

That ONE THING couldn't save her life

**33**[2]

      The gods pray for us, Dude says

The gods are in us, ol' guy says

We are gods, I say

But we forgot where we came from

One day

Our memories will come back to us

And we'll stand as tall as that lady

Even if all we have are our little things

Made of plastic and fake china and cracked wood

**34**

      I'm feeling dizzy now

Arms tense

---

[2] This chapter is optional, i.e. it may or may not be played in performance.

Legs spent

Stomach fulla cheese and soda

I forgot to eat right

I just walked out the door

Goin for a ride

Didn't know anything was gonna happen

Drone hovers

Hey, drone, help me out here

Do something for the world

Drone keeps flying

Headin over there, I bet

To where the real godforsaken mess is

I don't even wanna think about it

'cause the news?

The stuff over there?

Man oh man, it's like the stuff over here times a hundred

Mom and dad think I don't see the pictures

When they put the news on

They think I got my mind on toys n shit

But I see

**35**

      Like, that kid[3] sitting on that piece of cardboard

Next to the grocery store

They're always sitting there

In their black clothes

N stinky hair

Moving their head up n down

Making sounds their mouth

Like they're wailing or pleading

---

[3] The gender of this other kid is intentionally ambiguous, hence the use of "their."

Or just asking the light in the sky to send them peace

Nobody says anything

We all act like the kid's not there

Cuz the kid's always there

Always

A fixture, someone says

We got tired of trying to help

Don't want it anyway

Lazy

Don't wanna look for a job

The kid makes sounds

Moves their head up and down

Anxious

Crazy anxious

Making signs in the air

I wanna give the kid a dollar

Mom says,

    Get inside,

    Get in the car

    NOW

We drive away

Kid keeps moving their head up and down
Why can't I give them a dollar?

    That kid will just spend it on drugs

With a dollar?

    Be quiet now.

We ride in silence

I'm thinking of the kid n their stinky hair

And how they looked so young

We could be kin

Be quiet now

Who's to say?
Maybe somewhere down the line
We're blood or-

Be QUIET

I slam the door to my room when we get home
The dollar burns in my pocket
Next time, next time I'm gonna give
Don't care what anybody says

**36**

The air sings a song of reason
I'm feeling strangely hopeful

Maybe this is what happens when a person's crossed the divide


My body feels as light as air

My head is full of dreams

I'm thinking maybe tonight we will win the lottery

How cool would that be?


Not having to think anymore

'Bout what we need and what we're gonna do

Cuz we'll have everything


37


      Like the Guy

The one who owns half this town

People say he's evil

People call him all sorts of names


And yeah, he killed the trees

And yeah, he's don't really care 'bout us

And yeah, he's a big monster


But I saw him once

On the other side of town

Far, far away from his luxury condo

He was sitting in some little restaurant

All alone

Totally not the kind of place you'd expect him to be


Cuz this place was, like, little

Ten tables at most

With plastic placemats and plastic glasses

And day-old bread in the bread basket


He was eating a HUGE cake of a thing

I was, like, what the hell is that?


Quiche, a voice said


It was all yellow with bits of green and a weird crusty kind of edge

And it looked like it had been sitting in the freezer for a hella long time

He was wearing his suit

But it wasn't pressed

His face was puffy

His eyes were red

He kept looking at his phone

But not doing anything with it

Just looking

Staring

Picking at his quiche

He ordered a soda

HUGE soda

He slurped

Made noises

Looked at the phone

Asked the server for the time

I was, like, what'd he need it for?

He knows the time

It's on his phone

But he asked anyway

He wanted to hear someone's voice

Wanted someone to have the right answer when he asked a question

**38**

    I was sitting in the corner

I'd stopped in for a soda

Don't usually come by this part of town

Cuz everything here's slow and dull and smells of gasoline

Ol' guy says there was a factory here once that made cars

    I'm, like, uh-huh

Ol' guy says this part of town used to be happening

He uses that word "happening"

Like it got some special meaning

He laughs

Makes a gesture with his hands

Revels in his secret

I'd been riding past my usual time

I'd been trying to set a record

Not in some book

Just for myself

I figured if I was gonna be in the tour de France someday

I had to start training now

That day my goal had been two hundred miles

I know

I know

They usually do 2200 miles over 23 days


My goal was unrealistic

I know

I know, OKAY?


But if you don't set a goal, what's the point?

I'd put in about hundred miles

Between the flats and the hills

I was thirsty


When the restaurant


**39**


   Mom and dad had taken me there once

Way, way back

Maybe when I was five

They said it was kinda down home but real good

N we could totally get something authentic there

Didn't know what they meant by authentic
Cuz food is food, right?

But they said, this place has real food
Like in the ol' days
Nothing fancy but it will fill you up

The tables are fake wood
And full of stains that won't go away

The chairs make you slide
Like, they got something on 'em

The floor is dark n unsteady
Swear you feel you're gonna fall down
If you don't look where you're going
I'm not sure about this place
But mom and dad say, it's good, you'll see
Besides, we drove all this way, didn't we?

They got chicken pot pies and mashed potatoes

I got an omelet that tasted like beans

Big tall sodas and cold cups of coffee

**40**

    I am full, the Guy said

As he finished the last bite of his quiche

I was downing my soda

Like I'd raced 'cross the Pyrenees

Guy was looking at his phone

He sees me

*Red bike, red bike*

And then he starts crying

Flat out bawling like a child

I'm thinking, if he wants-

But no

Cuz he turns his phone over

Puts his head in his hands

And keeps crying

There's hardly anyone in the little restaurant

The server pretends to pay him no mind

People do things like this all the time in places like these, I hear someone say

It's coming from the front

The cash register

Person behind it looks all of ten

But they're way older than that

They have fake braids and a funny smile

And they're standing behind the register

Like it's a fort

"People do things like that all the time"

I wanna smack them

I'm not violent
I'm not prone, as they say
But sometimes this kinda feeling comes over me
And it makes me wanna do things
Really bad things

Don't you see this guy's crying?

I bet he's cheating on somebody, person says
And gives a customer their change

I walk over to the cash register
Stare at the person
They look startled

I pull at their fake, store-bought, stupid, dangling braid

Person slaps my hand

Guy stops crying

Looks at us

Looks at me

**41**

      Jump on the bike

Start pedaling as fast as my legs will let

Hear his voice in my brain

*Red bike, red bike, red bike*

I am flying

No way is he

No hella way is he gonna take this bike away from me

My mom and dad paid good money for this bike

It is mine

All mine

What's he want with it anyway?

He owns half the town already

Greedy sonofabitch

Go cry in someone else's quiche

LEAVE ME THE HELL ALONE

*Red bike, red bike, red bike*

His voice won't let up

I am racing

Pushing against myself

Flats and hills

Curves and rivulets

I'm steering like one of them Olympic dudes

Total gold medal shit

Past the warehouse

Past the Waffle Stop

Past the silo

I am an animal now

Made of skin and bone

Air and light


My body is one with the bike


*Red, red, red*


I am singing a chord of happiness

I'm bleeding joy

Look out, world

LOOK OUT


**42**

      Something greasy

Losing control

The sky's in my face

The ground is nowhere to be found

I am in some kinda cloud

Legs moving

But I can't feel anything

Arms tensin up

Veins and muscle

The Waffle Stop sign is far away now

The silo is a postcard from long ago

I see a feather floating outta the corner of my eye

It's the color of sadness

Color of motion

Flecks of blue, grey and aquamarine

I'm sinking into my chest

Falling into a dream

*Red, red, red*

The Guy's face is covered in leaves

He moves like a monster

He is a monster

How'd he get here?

Why's he following me?

I try to pedal with all of my might

But I can't feel my feet

*Red, red, red*

I'm like one of those kids on the news

From that place far, far away

Weighed down by a desire for forgiveness

My lips are smarting, cracking from the heat

My teeth are numb

My cheeks are drowning in tears

I'm beyond a cartoon on TV

I'm beyond everything

I think of mom and dad

Waiting for me

I think of Dude and their two-dollar dreams

I think of ol' Guy and how he also talks about winning the lottery

I see numbers on a card

Could this be how we make something out of our lives?

The monster rustles

The air is thick

I think about how everyone's in a hurry these days

How nobody says I'm sorry

How people don't know how to talk to one other

How everybody's robbed of sleep

The monster stares

His eyes are gone

Just sockets now

Just the burning ash of leaves

*Red, red, red*

He has something in his hand

Can't make it out

Something shiny

Points it at me

Laughs

But it sounds like a cry

Like someone in the worst kinda pain ever

*Red, red, red*

**43**

    I'm dreaming of a house

Way out in the country

The house is made of all sorts of things

Patched together from years of living

I walk into it

Except I have no feet

I float

My torso is the body of the bike

My arms hang at my sides

He won't find me here

This place is far, far away

Years from now

Beyond his imagining

The house lifts me into its arms

Cradles me like a child

It smells of old paint and moss and summers by the sea

I want to touch its walls

But it whispers something

I fall asleep

**44**

    My mom works in the clinic part time
People speak to her in broken languages
They ask her to make things better, please

They have coins in their pockets
And dig dollars out from the soles of their shoes
They say if you tell us we're okay
If you put it down in ink
We can get a job
A better job
One that will get us one step closer to the lottery

My mom asks them to fill out forms
She has the patience of ten gods
She listens to them

And holds her breath

And doesn't let on to anyone

That she has the same dreams they do

This land is not mine

This land is not yours

This land is just land

**45**

    The monster breathes

*Red, red*

He looks inside the house

Through the window out front

There's the stench of old water

Coming from the backyard

There's the sound of a party

Moving through the trees

This used to be a theater once, a voice sings

This used to be parlor

This used to be a ballroom

The monster wheezes

Crumpling his body against the front of the house

He lets the shiny thing fall from his hands

He's not run this far this fast in a long time

He misses the sky

He misses the things he knows

*Stocks and derivatives and securities*

His voice is like a green stem

As he lets out another cry

And bangs his fists against the door of the house

I think to open it

But the house won't let me

The house has got me by the arms

And it won't let go

He says the future has no time for voices from the past

Especially voices

That wheeze and needle and cry

I struggle in the house's arms

I've never been one for shelter

I long for the road

And the hill

The rivulets and the winding curves

And the way flats become hills become flats again

I tell the house that if the monster wants to see me

I'm ready for him

Even if I can't tear down the sign that says FOR LEASE


The house caresses my steel torso

It kisses my aluminum arms

It rests its hands on my bones threaded with carbon fiber


Go on now, it says

Go for a ride

See ya later


**46**

    There's a part of the road that smells like fire

I warm to it

Like the breath of the ancients


The shiny thing sticks in the mud

As the monster wheezes

His last days

*Red, red*

I feel blessed

Strange

In the old books that people read once long ago

It was said monsters ate through the better part of you

So that you could find the rest of your way

Drone hovers

I let the fire lick my tongue

Red, red

The city sleeps in a yellow haze

Blue shutters snap against the faint breeze

The silo glows in the distance

Steel aluminum carbon fiber

Courses through my veins

Legs feel the weight of tomorrow

Arms feel the shudder of yesterday


The shiny thing barely glints

As the monster reaches for it


A parade of laughter

A litany of red


    It's a fork, he says

    It's nothing but a fork

    Is this what you're running from, kid?

The Guy is standing

Suit pressed

His hand a phone

The fork dangles from his pocket


I was eating a quiche, he says to the air

I catch him smiling

Wondering if I'll give him a smile back

Hot

    Yes

Way it is here

Way it always is in summer

I have half a mind to turn back

But I can't find my feet

I left them back at the house

Guy keeps staring

The fork dangles on the edge of his right pocket

Who says I'm running?

    Sorry?

I'm not running from anybody

You're a funny kid

You're not getting my bike

And then he raises his arms

Like a monster genuine bonafide

Tall, tall up to the sky

The fork in his right hand

Gleaming of quiche

From when he bit on it last

He looks like he's coming toward me

But he's not moving his legs

He's planted on the ground

His shoes dusty from the road and the heat

Did you steal that fork?

Are you a thief?

His arms get longer, higher into the sky

Cracking through the heavens

They'll make you pay for it

He laughs
Loud, big and rumbly
Like a perfect cartoon monster

Except the laugh
Got another note inside
That rings hollow, sad and strange

I stand my ground
Even without feet

Are you a thief?

His laugh becomes an ocean
Steel and glass and cascades of numbers
Pour from it

He moves toward me

For real this time

Are you?

*Red, red, red*

I think now is the time to pull out my superhero moves

Now is the time to turn into a beast

Or something with a cape

But I am frozen

My superhero signals aren't firing anything to my brain

Guy aims the fork at the universe

Like he's about to give a proclamation

    I AM WHAT YOU MADE ME

And with these words

With these simple words

The fork comes down

Straight

Into my heart

His laughter enters my body

His outsized arms engulf me

    I AM WHAT YOU MADE ME

**47**

    I think of our town

Our little town

Stuck in the middle of nowhere

Poised for majesty

There were fields and fields of corn and wheat

The Ol' Guy said

And now there are just warehouses full of stuff

What are we gonna do?

What are we gonna do with all that stuff?

The bus ambles down the road

A road that's not even a highway

I try to imagine the corn

I try to imagine the wheat

I pretend I'm in some movie

Camera sweeping through vast fields of glory

Nature electric in its bloom

But my imagination fails me

As the bus squawks and hisses to a stop

N ol' guy says,

>We're running low on gas
>
>Gotta fill up

I sit in the bus

Waiting

Thinking about nothing and everything

I was born into this

Why's ol' guy blamin me?

Pure sad, he says

        Things that happen now are pure sad

What's he want from me?

I can't fix sadness

Hell, I'm no good with corn and wheat

I need stuff

We all do

Don't we?

My dad needs that job

If that warehouse weren't there,

We'd be starving

'cause it's that job, that job that keeps us going

'cause the other nine jobs he's got don't add up to one


Ol' Guy's dreaming

Bout some past that's never comin' back

Pure sad, he mutters


Ground wouldn't remember how to grow corn and wheat

All it knows now is concrete

Steel and glass

**48**


    My arteries smell of eggs and broccoli

The fork wedges into the membrane of my heart

The monster laughs

As I sputter onto the baking heat of the road


*I am what you made me*

I see him walk over to my bike

*Red, red*

He lifts it gingerly onto his arms
Light as a feather

He cries a solemn cry
That sounds as if he is praying

*Chaos reieieieieieigns*

As he hurls it down the hill
Down to the edge of the city
Past the trees
And the fields
And the small houses clinging to the earth

Crash

The bike hits a massive wall

A splatter of red limbs

Against grey concrete

Wheels, gears, spokes

Scatter their remains

Onto an ocean of gravel


The sound is small

Gentle, almost

An innocent crash


As the monster walks away

And I struggle to breathe


**49**


    In the dictionary

A bike is described as a human-powered

Pedal-driven

Single-track vehicle

Having two wheels

Attached to a frame,

One behind the other

Its motion depends on us

Where we go? It follows


But what happens when we don't know where we're going?

What happens when all we can think of is the bike?


When I was six I wanted to be a helicopter

I wanted to hover

Like a drone

Over the earth

And be able to swoop down and see things up close


I wanted to rescue people

And fly in combat

Like I'd seen in the movies

I wanted to do good


My mom and dad said human beings can't be helicopters

And that I should delete that idea from my list of dreams

Be realistic, they said

Think of practical things


So, I thought of all of the things

I saw people do in this town


Like, mow the lawn

Do drugs

Crash parties

Smoke weed

Go to church

Marry

Have babies

Get into fist fights


Go to jail

Go to the movies

Watch TV

Watch their screens

Watch football

Watch baseball

Watch basketball

Watch wrestling

Watch anything

Watch everything

Cuss at their children

Wail at their grandparents

Cry over commercials

Beat each other up

        to be first in line at a shopping spree

Sit on the lawn

Watch the fireworks

Pray

This land is not mine

This land is not yours

This land is just land

And then

Shoot a gun into the air

For fun

For kicks

For love

For hate

For nothing

For nothing

Just to shoot

Just to be

Say I am here

I was here

Someone made me

And then roar

Like animals

Cry

Like babies

Think of the past

Of the rain

Of the days when

People loved each other

And didn't think about things

Like stuff

Stuff they needed

'cause someone said

If they didn't have

If they didn't need

They were nothing

Nothing

Without their stuff

And no one

No one

Wants to be nothing

NO ONE

NO ONE

WANTS TO BE NOTHING

So we became our stuff

And we thought nothing of it

Because it was chaos

And it tasted good

Sweet

Like candy

Like skittles and rocks and jelly beans

And our teeth rotted

And our mouths stayed open

And our bellies grew

And our tongues licked the edges of everything

Even when we prayed

Even when we said grace

Until we forgot

We forgot what it is that we wanted

We forgot that the only thing we were here for

Is to learn how to live

And learn how to die

**50**

The neon sign buzzes in my ear

My mouth is on the edge of the road

Next to the Waffle Stop

> Bad turn, someone says
> You took a bad turn on the road

I reach for the fork stuck in my heart

But there is nothing

Except for a tiny gash

I reach to one side to get up

My feet are aching

What time is…?

I can barely make out the words

Everything is slow and blurry

> Supper, someone says
> You comin' in for a waffle?
> You got kin?

I look at the faded blue streaks dancing in the sky

I think if I don't get home,

Mom and dad will be worried sick all night

I'm all right.

    You sure?

I start walking

The sun has gone down

The heat has faded

My clothes are sticky, smelly,

N stained with gravel and dirt

I think: I need to get my moves back

Or I am never gonna make the tour de France

When a voice says

    This your bike?

I see it

Over there

Leaning sideways

Against the faded stem

Of the Waffle Stop sign

Red bike

It stares at me the same way it did once

From behind the store window

      This yours?

I think of Ol' Guy working the late shift on the bus

I think of Dude making their little songs on the drums

I think of how this town may be shit

But it's all we got

And how sometimes

Sometimes

I like feeling like a superstar

Even though I know I'm just a kid

And by the time I'm twelve

My dreams are hella gonna change

And by the time I'm the same age as Ol' Guy

    If I get there

I'll have seen so much of the world

I'll wonder how it is one can hold all of that inside

Without making some serious NOISE


Voice says again,

    This your bike?


Yes.


And I ride away

Into the night.


*End of play*

About the Author:

Caridad Svich received a 2012 OBIE Award for Lifetime Achievement in the theatre, a 2017-18 Visiting Fellow at Royal Central School of Speech and Drama, a 2012 Edgerton Foundation New Play Award and NNPN rolling world premiere for *Guapa*, and the 2011 American Theatre Critics Association Primus Prize for her play *The House of the Spirits*, based Isabel Allende's novel. She has been short-listed for the PEN Award in Drama four times. Key works in her repertoire include *12 Ophelias, Iphigenia Crash Land Falls on the Neon Shell That Was Once Her Heart, Fugitive Pieces, Alchemy of Desire/Dead-Man's Blues, The Way of Water, and RED BIKE*. She has also adapted for the stage novels by Mario Vargas Llosa, Julia Alvarez and Jose Leon Sanchez, and has radically reconfigured works from Wedekind, Euripides, Sophocles, and Shakespeare. As a theatrical translator she has translated nearly all the plays of Federico Garcia Lorca, and works by Lope de Vega, Calderon de la Barca, and contemporary works from Spain, Mexico and Cuba. She has also edited several books on theatre and performance, among them *Fifty Playwrights on Their Craft* (Methuen Drama, 2017) and *Audience Revolution* (TCG, 2016). She is published by Intellect Books, Seagull Books, Broadway Play Publishing, Manchester University Press, Smith & Kraus and Playscripts. She is alumna playwright of New Dramatists, contributing editor of *Contemporary Theatre Review*, drama editor of *Asymptote* literary translation journal, contributing editor of *TheatreForum* and an affiliated artist of EST, Lark and New Georges, and is founder of NoPassport theatre alliance and press. Website: http://www.caridadsvich.com